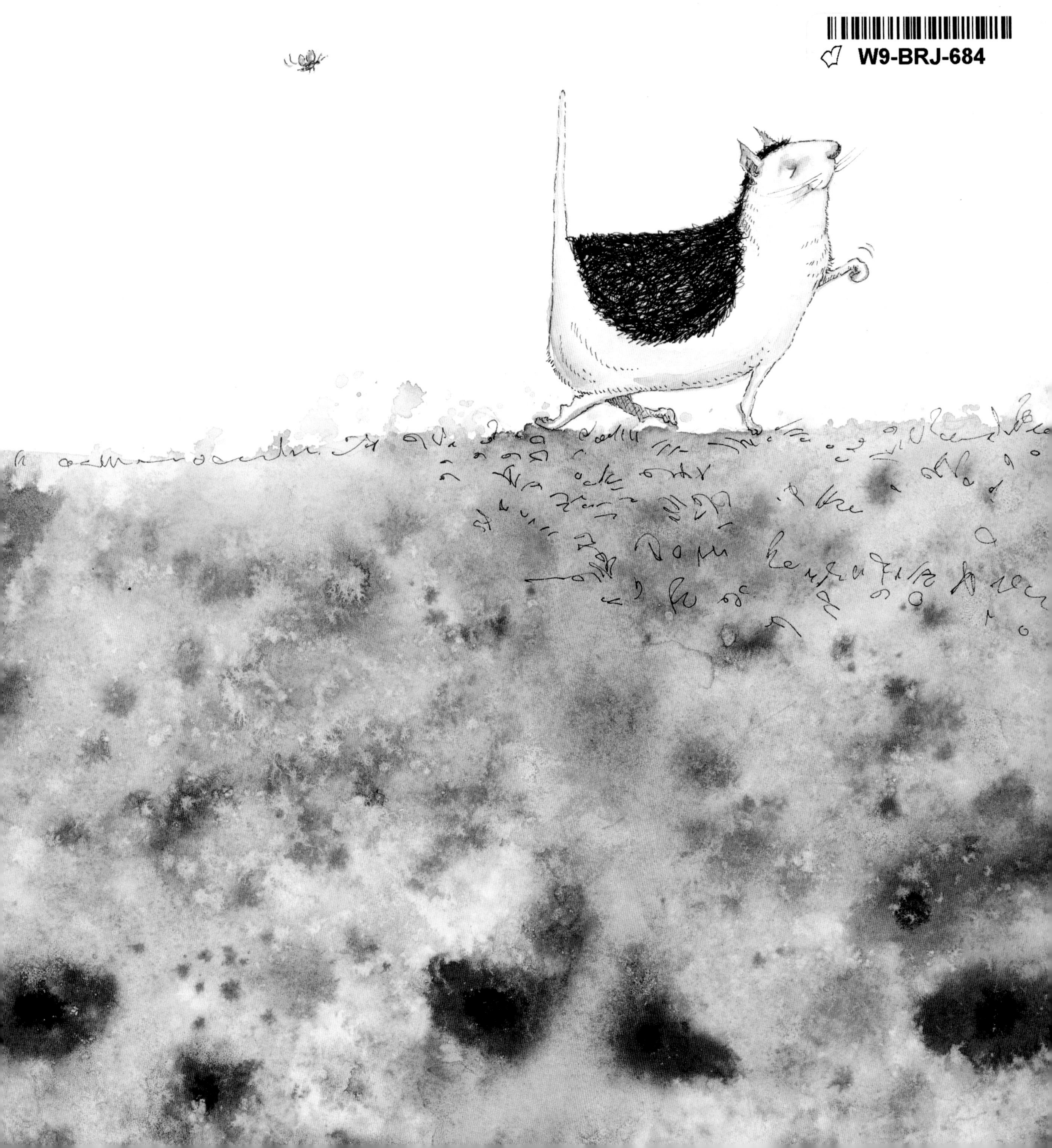

Blue Ethel

JENNIFER BLACK REINHARDT

MARGARET FERGUSON BOOKS
FARRAR STRAUS GIROUX
NEW YORK

Ethel was old.

She was fat.

She was black.

She was white.

And she was very
set in her ways.

Every day Ethel went outside to survey the land,

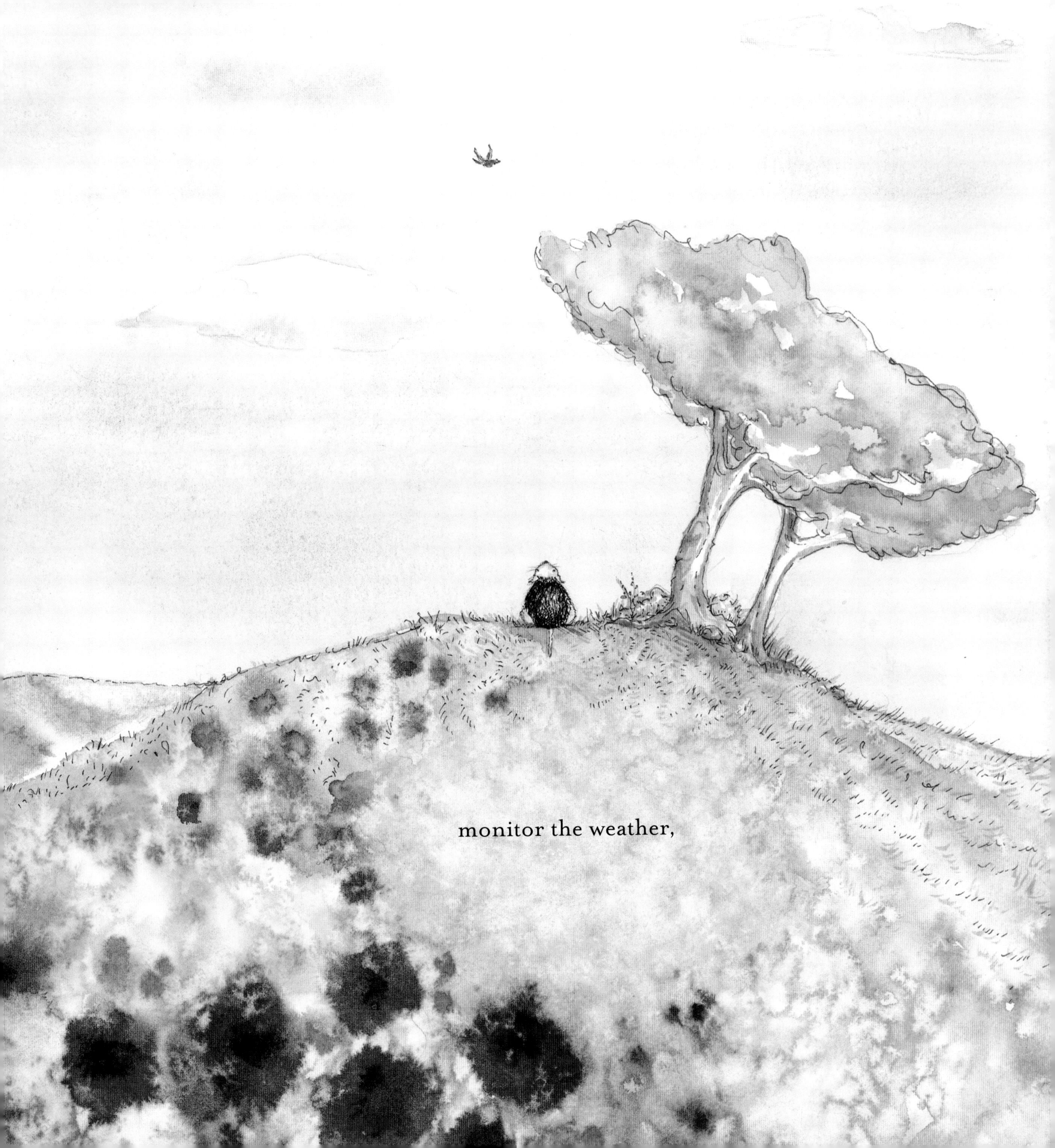

monitor the weather,

chase villains,

and explore her favorite sidewalk square, where she liked to roll before taking a nap after her long day.

It wasn't easy being Ethel, but she was good at it.

Until late one afternoon . . .

After she rolled

and rolled

and rolled,

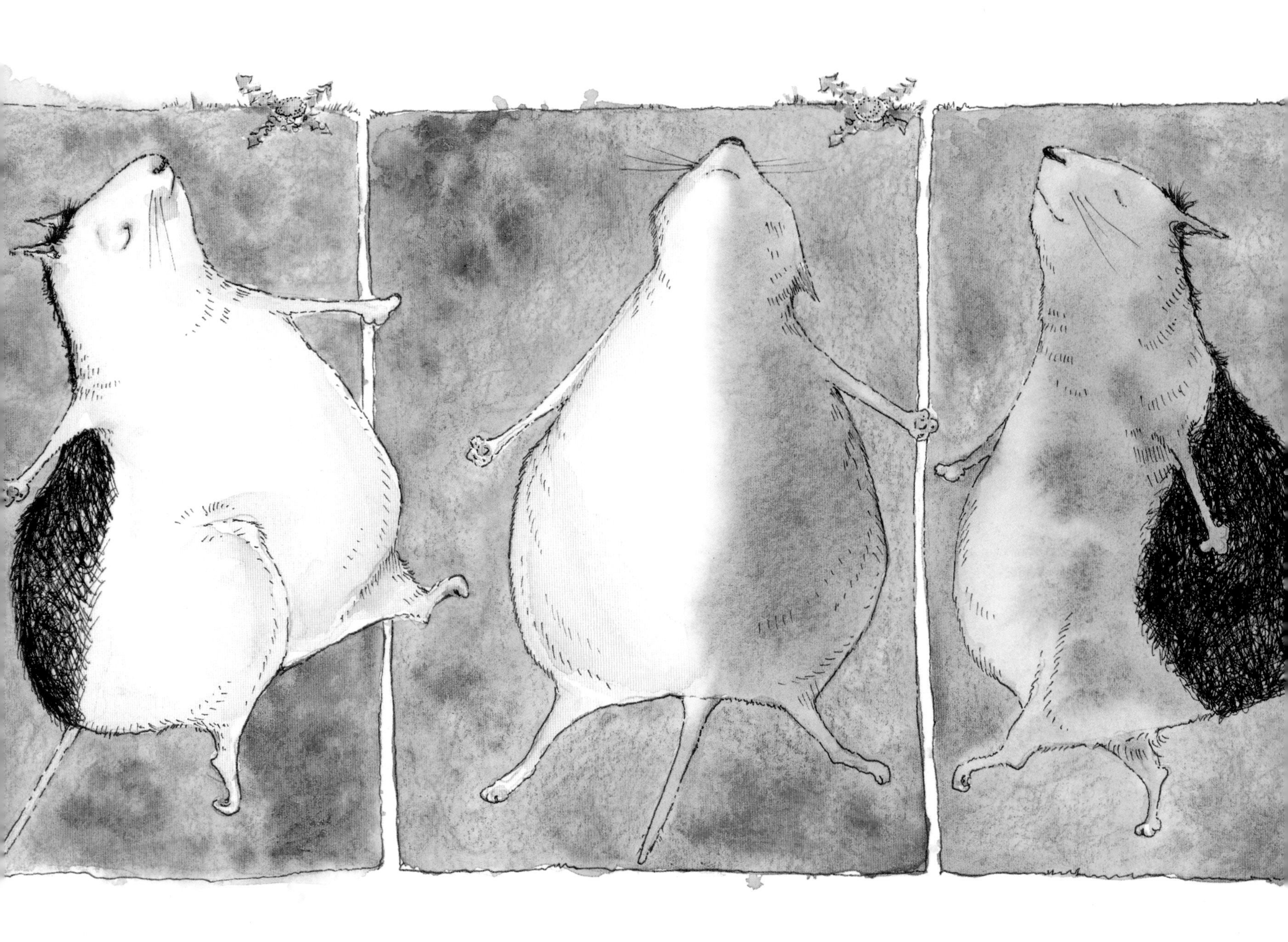

Ethel was still old.
She was still fat.
She was still black.
But Ethel was no longer white.

Ethel didn't know it, but she was . . .

BLUE.

WAS
THERE
ARE

On her way home that evening, Ethel
noticed others looking at her strangely.

Then she heard whispers.

"Azure!"

"Cerulean!"

"Cobalt!"

"How odd!"

"How interesting!"

"Ethel's blue!"

Ethel's heart sank to her paws.
She wasn't supposed to be blue.
And it made her feel very, very

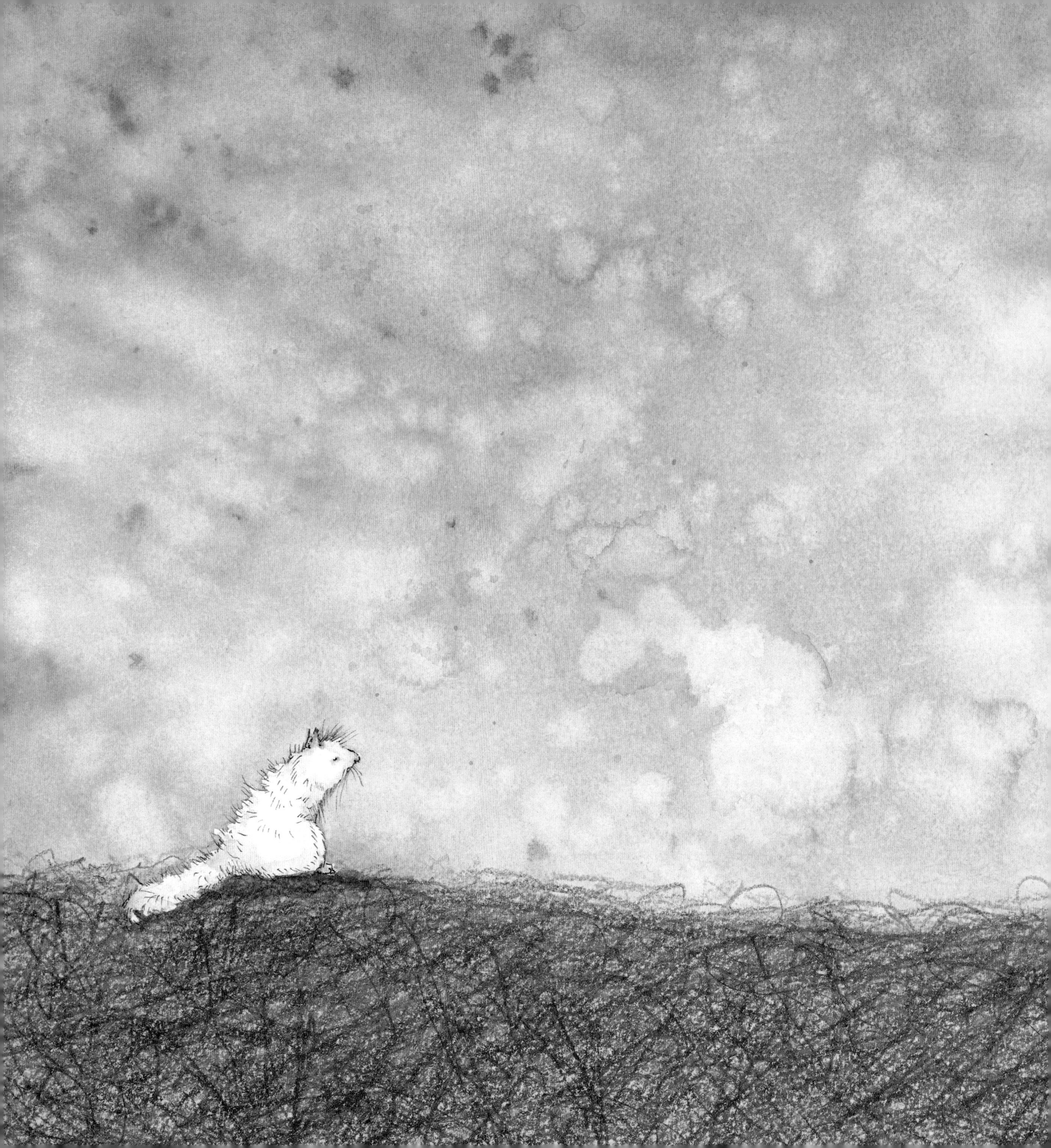

BLUE.

SOIL
Garden

ETHEL
YARD
TUNA
FISH

The next morning, Ethel felt too blue to go outside.

She looked out the window
and saw Fluffy, who was young,
and slim, and usually white.

But today he was . . .

PINK.

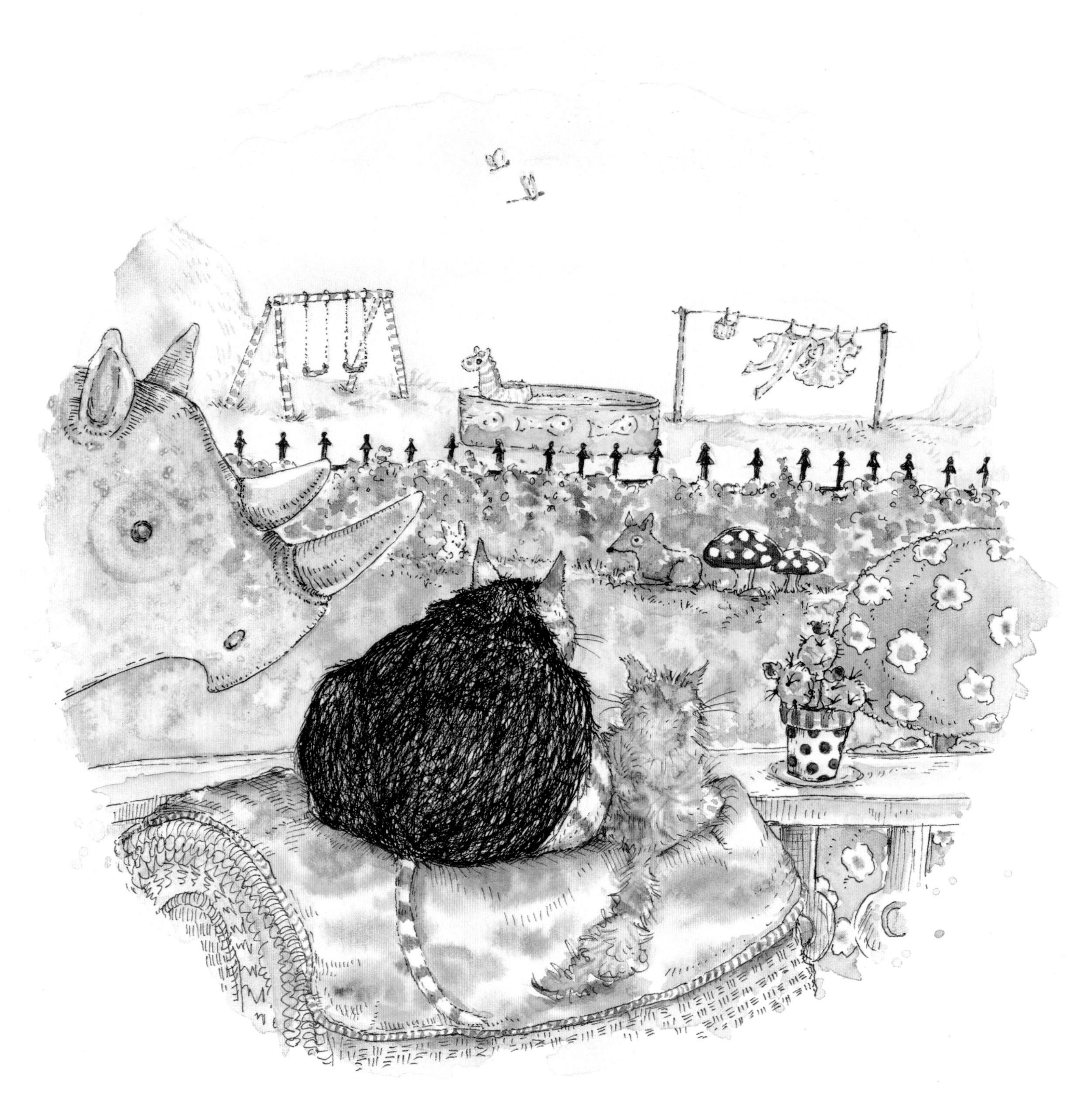

Together they surveyed the land,

monitored the weather,

and chased villains.

And when they explored the sidewalk
square, they rolled and rolled and
rolled and became . . .

COLORFUL.

Ethel was still old.
She was still fat.
She was still black.
And some days she was still white . . .
unless another color caught her fancy.

It wasn't easy being Ethel, but she was good at it.

This book is dedicated to Ethel,
and to all who have known and loved her.
And to Ashley and Eliza—the artists.
—J.B.R.

Farrar Straus Giroux Books for Young Readers
An imprint of Macmillan Publishing Group, LLC
175 Fifth Avenue, New York 10010

Color separations by Bright Arts (H.K.) Ltd.
Printed in China by Toppan Leefung Printing Ltd.,
Dongguan City, Guangdong Province
First edition, 2017
1 3 5 7 9 10 8 6 4 2

mackids.com

Library of Congress Cataloging-in-Publication Data

Names: Reinhardt, Jennifer Black, 1963– author, illustrator.
Title: Blue ethel / Jennifer Black Reinhardt.
Description: First edition. | New York : Margaret Ferguson Books/Farrar Straus Giroux, 2017. |
Summary: "Ethel the cat is surprised when, in the course of her usual day, she unexpectedly turns blue"— Provided by publisher.
Identifiers: LCCN 2016035845 | ISBN 9780374303822 (hardback)
Subjects: | CYAC: Cats—Fiction. | Change—Fiction. |
Self-confidence—Fiction. | BISAC: JUVENILE FICTION / Animals / Cats.
Classification: LCC PZ7.R276 Bl 2017 | DDC [E]—dc23
LC record available at https://lccn.loc.gov/2016035845